Police Cow
and
Road Safety School

for Dania and Oleksiy, my beloved boys

Written by:

HELEN POLI

Illustrated by:

ASIA SHOOKATY

In the small town of Olliville there live many animals of different kinds: big and serious animal-grown-ups and little carefree animal-kids. As they should, all the grown-ups go to work every day, have rest on weekends and spend their vacation at the sea from time to time. All kids lead a happy kids' life: they play a lot, make big noises, sometimes study and act polite at times, as kids should.

Our story will be about a cow whose name is Ruby and who works for this town's police. You might say, " What a wonder, how come a cow has suddenly become a police officer; could she even fit into a police car?"

But as you know, all dreams come true in this world. And if you for some reason can't fit into the police car, there may be something else for you.

So it happened. Ruby became a police cow. She patrolled the town in a special police bus and was the happiest cow in the town.

There is not much work for a police officer in Olliville. All animals live in peace and friendship.

Miss Ruby's biggest concern is chicks. For some reason they can't memorize the traffic rules. They refuse to go on the sidewalks and ignore crosswalks. Miss Police Officer has even written tickets to the parents of some chicks. It lasted them for several days and then they made a fresh start—the little mischief-makers have been all over the place again. The traffic on the town's roads is slowed down; the cars honk all the time trying to drive in between the chicks.

Our Ruby has had enough of it, so eventually she decided to solve this problem once and for all. She settled on a meadow near the police station, and closed her eyes to think.

The first idea that came to her mind was this—to place signs along the road that would warn drivers to slow down because there may be chicks on the road.

"No! Everyone knows about it anyway. It won't do!" Miss Ruby exclaimed to herself.

"Maybe I should prohibit the chicks from leaving home? Oh, The parents would hate that idea!" Ruby went on reflecting.

At last, something looked like a good option:

"What if I set up a school of traffic safety where we could teach both chicks and other kids the rules of traffic on the town's roads? Maybe it'll work well?"

Inspired by her idea, Ruby rushed to the fire station where Cat Turly, an old friend of our cow, worked as a fire officer.

"Turly, I've got it! I came up with a great idea!" Ruby called to her friend-fire officer, still on her way.

"What's up? What fire are you escaping from?" Mister Turly asked.

"You dream of fires everywhere, Turly. There is no flame. I have found the way to cope with the chickens' mess in our town! We can't forbid them going out to the streets but we are quite capable of teaching them the traffic rules. Let's organize a school of traffic safety. We'll call it something like 'Turlyruby' or 'Rubyturly", Ruby chattered as quickly as she could.

"What an inventor you are Ruby, turlyruby, rubyturly, murlymyrly moo moo miaow," Turly laughed in response.

"So, you won't help? You think it's a bad idea?"

"I'm just joking, the idea is great!" Turly replied. "May I also be a teacher?"

"Yes! Sure! You're the best friend in the world!" Ruby was delighted and hugged her buddy.

This is how our friends have started organizing a traffic school.

The easiest part was to find the place. And as the summer reigned in the town, Cat and Ruby decided to set up the school

at a large lawn next to the police station. Turly painted a big colorful poster with the inscription "Super School of Road Safety." After that he and Ruby installed it at the lawn's entrance.

All of the next day Ruby has been driving down the streets of the town. Miss Police Officer announced the school opening in the loudspeaker and invited all kids to the new school:

"Attention please!!! To all townspeople of Olliville! Tomorrow on the lawn near the police station the Super School of Road Safety for kids will be opening! All kids and their parents are invited! See you there!"

The next morning Ruby and Turly have come to their school early looking forward to greeting the first pupils. Miss Police Officer was very worried that nobody would come and constantly checked time by her watch. But Turly was calm and joked all morning: "Ruby! Turly! Moo moo miaow!"

By the fixed time the kids and the parents began to gather on the lawn, most of all the moms-hens with their chicks have come.

The animals were taking places on the grass and waited for the classes to start. Very soon the whole lawn was packed with the students of the new school.

The class started with the speech by Mister Turly who has told the kids and their parents about his concern: how it's difficult for cars to drive through if pedestrians don't follow the traffic rules; that, apart from slowing down the traffic, it poses a threat to the kids themselves who can simply get under the wheels of a car.

"That would be terrible!" one of the chicks exclaimed.

After this introduction Turly has asked Ruby to speak and she has started training. First of all, Miss Police Officer explains the difference between a sidewalk and a road to the kids:

"Only vehicles can go down the road. Those who move around the town on their 2 or 4 legs are called pedestrians and must only go down the sidewalks. That's you! If a pedestrian needs to cross the street, he must use a crosswalk which is marked with such a sign." Ruby has shown the pictures prepared in advance to the kids.

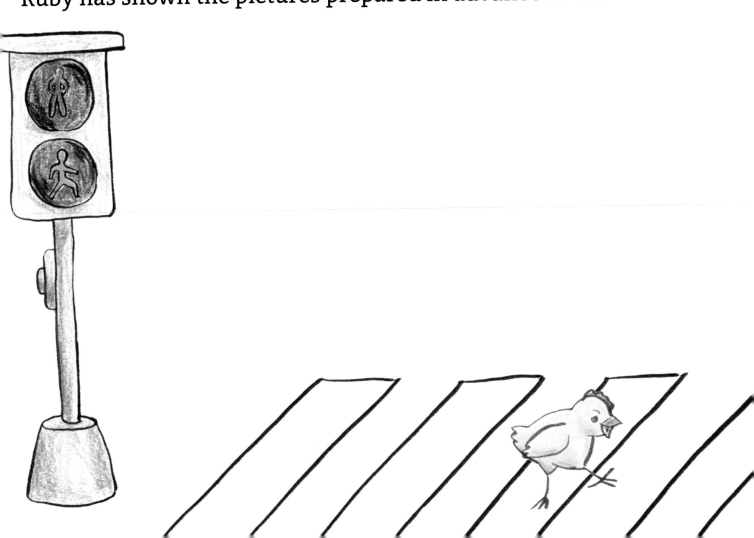

"Apart from the sign, a crosswalk is also marked with white ripes on the road similar to zebra's stripes," Miss Cow continues.

"There is one more important rule. You should cross the street th grown-ups, always holding their paw or wing. Before each ossing of the road you should stop and look both ways to check there is a car. Today you will even have the first homework to do. hen our lesson is over, I want every family attending the classes get home only using sidewalks and crosswalks."

Having finished the story about crosswalks, Miss Ruby has invited the kids to ask questions.

The chick Kerry was the first to raise his small wing. "May we have a ride on the fire truck?"

"Yes! Yes! May we? May we? When???" Tens of kids' voices have resounded repeating the most important kids' question.

"Dear kids, the classes aren't over yet. Tomorrow we'll have another lesson at our school."

"And tomorrow, will they take us for a ride?" Kerry didn't quiet down.

"I guess Mister Turly will take all those who so desire for a ride.

n't forget to do the homework. See you tomorrow morning, bye-e!" Miss Ruby finished the lesson.

The next morning Mister Fire Officer is giving classes at school. He has even got a set of lights somewhere which burned a green, a yellow and a red light in turn.

"Here, kids, is an extremely important helper on the street for both grown-up drivers and little pedestrians. By its signals we know when to cross the street and when to stop and wait. The lights for pedestrians only have 2 signals: red and green. The red little man means that you can't cross the street now; the green little man means that you can go.

"The traffic lights for vehicles have 3 colors: in addition to the red and the green signals, there is also the yellow one which means that the colors of the traffic lights are about to change.

"There are very many other things which we have to learn, kiddies. But first Miss Ruby and I want to teach you about moving with safe routes and making life easier for the drivers of our town Turly added.

"And now let's all go to Miss Ruby, she'll give you all the nice badges showing that you have had the first classes at our school!

"When you get them, come back to me, I'll wait for you at the e truck!"

"And we'll ride it???" The kids have started calling from all les.

"Get the badges and I will be waiting for you! I'll tell and show u what's here and how it works," Mister Fire Officer answered.

For a long time Miss Ruby has been waiting for the kids with the ɪdges, which featured a little traffic light.

"Oh! These badges are so nice!" The Kerry was the first one in ɪe line to receive such a beautiful present.

When done with receiving the badges, the kids surrounded th
fire truck of Mister Turly. He has allowed them all in turn to take h
seat in the truck and has driven a small round on the road next to
the police station.

And finally, while the kids clapped loudly, Mister Turly has
watered with the fire hose a small flowerbed nearby.

So have the studies at the traffic safety school come to an
end. All the kids went home holding on to their parents and using
sidewalks and crosswalks.

With the help of the parents the kids were making out the ɡnals of traffic lights and crossing the streets safely.

"Yay, I did it! Officer Ruby will be so proud of me!" Kerry the ick safely got home.

Ruby and Turly were incredibly happy that day. They knew ey had done something very important. Of course, they still have give many more lessons but from now on life in Olliville will be uch safer.

Ruby! **Turly!**

Moo! Moo!

Miaow!

Bye-bye!

HELEN POLI
Police Cow and Road Safety School

Made in United States
Orlando, FL
09 June 2022

18644307R00015